I'm a UNICORN

By Mallory C. Loehr
Illustrated by Joey Chou

A GOLDEN BOOK • NEW YORK

Text copyright © 2018 by Mallory C. Loehr.
Cover and interior illustrations copyright © 2018 by Joey Chou.
All rights reserved. Published in the United States by Golden Books, an imprint
of Random House Children's Books, a division of Penguin Random House LLC,
1745 Broadway, New York, NY 10019, and in Canada by Penguin Random House
Canada Limited, Toronto. Golden Books, A Golden Book, A Little Golden Book,
the G colophon, and the distinctive gold spine are registered trademarks
of Penguin Random House LLC.
rhcbooks.com
Educators and librarians, for a variety of teaching tools, visit us at
RHTeachersLibrarians.com
Library of Congress Control Number: 2(
ISBN 978-1-5247-1512-0 (trade) — ISBN 978-1-
Printed in the United States of Am

10

D1378216

I am moonlight white.
I have a magical horn.
I look a lot like a horse, of course.

I'm a UNICORN!

My horn can make water clean . . .

. . . or heal a hurt.

I can be strong and fierce.

I can be sweet and gentle.

I frolic in the forest.

I prance
in the fields.

I am a force of nature—

I'm a UNICORN!

Sometimes I gallop
with my herd.

We play hide-and-seek.

Can you find us all?

Other times,
I love to be alone

in the quiet of dawn.
Shhh. . . .

I am magic.
I am mystery.

I'm a
UNICORN!

Do you believe in me?

I believe in you!